# Helen Nicoll & Jan Pie

# QUEST FOR THE GLOOP

## Murfy & PHIX

**PUFFIN BOOKS**

Like a shimmering mirage the pyramid glides silently towards them

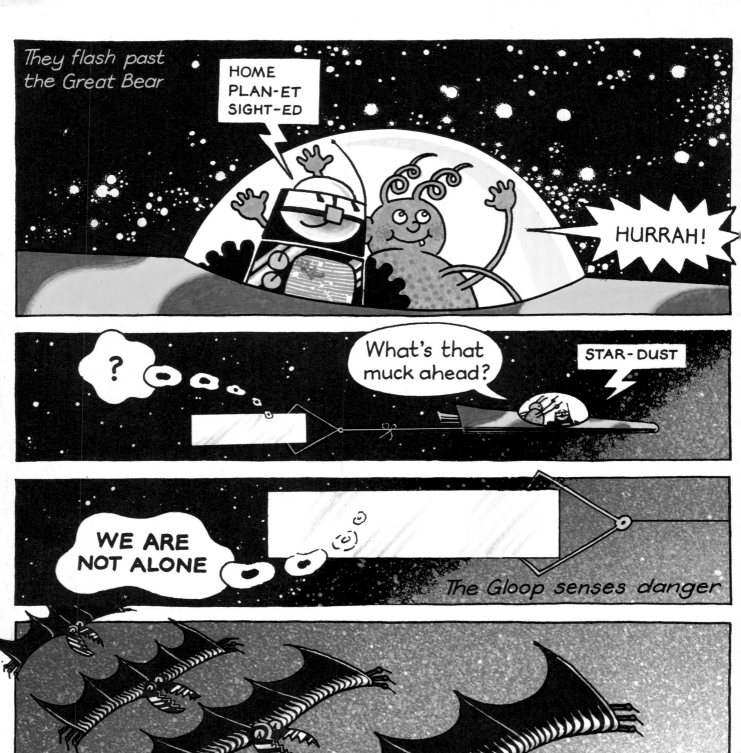

They flash past the Great Bear

HOME PLAN-ET SIGHT-ED

HURRAH!

?

What's that muck ahead?

STAR-DUST

WE ARE NOT ALONE

The Gloop senses danger

NIGHT FIGHTERS OF THE EMPRESS OF DARKNESS

What **are** they?

ROB-OT BATS

The surviving bat robot
limps home with the news

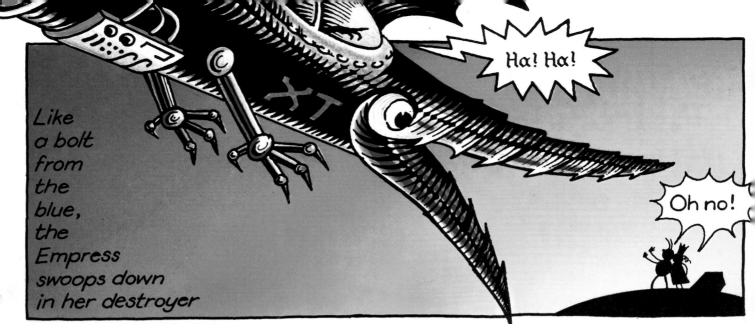

Like a bolt from the blue, the Empress swoops down in her destroyer

Ha! Ha!

Oh no!

SNAP!

Knock knock

WHO'S THERE?

Ida

I-DA WHO?

Ida feeling we'd see **her** again

ha ha

Now Captain, we must free the Gloop

Aye aye Highness

Find a power source PHIX

Begin warming up exercise

CONN-EC-TION LOC-AT-ED

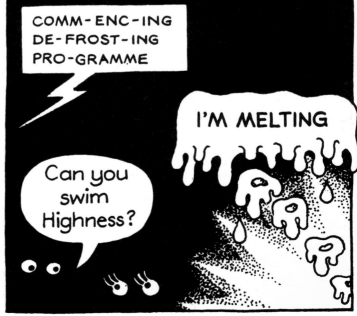

COMM-ENC-ING DE-FROST-ING PRO-GRAMME

I'M MELTING

Can you swim Highness?

Below on Beetlejuice 8, hope fades

Z Z Z Z Z Z

She thinks it's night all day

Hens don't lay

...it was for the Princess's birthday

We live in difficult times

Plants wilt

No grass

No milk

No breakfast

Cows give up

Suddenly a ray of light pierces the gloom

It's a star

It's a rocket

It's THE GLOOP!

The night watch on the palace roof are the first to see the light

The End